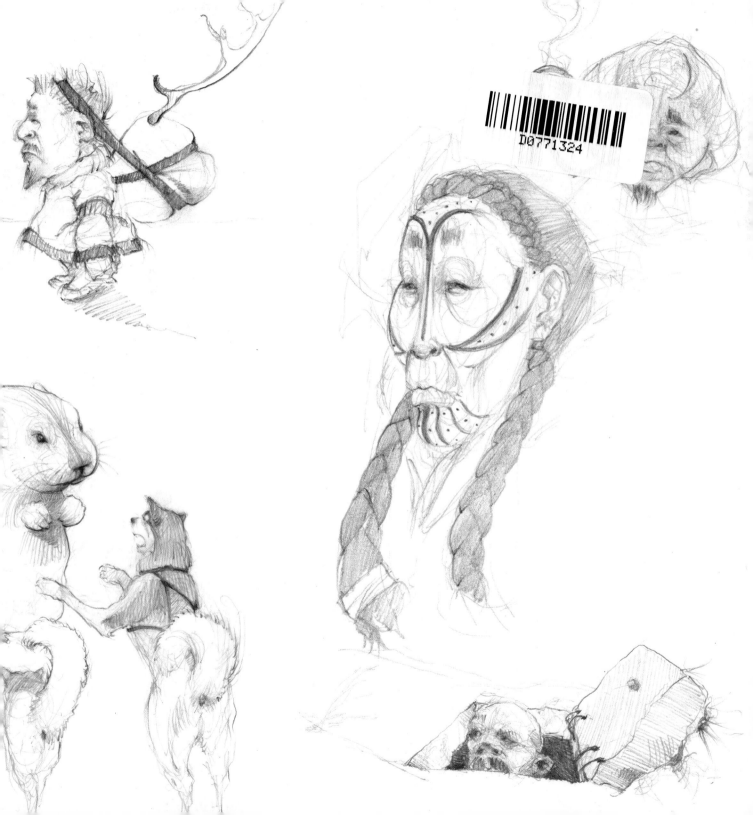

AVA
and the
LITTLE FOLK

AVA and the LITTLE FOLK

Written by

Neil Christopher and
Alan Neal

Illustrated by

Jonathan Wright

Introduction

If you visited storytellers across the Arctic and listened carefully to their tales, you would encounter an oral history filled with fantastic stories about incredible people, great journeys, strange beings, and supernatural creatures. Elders might share folktales about dangerous tribes of people or shape-shifting animals. You might stumble upon accounts of frightening monsters and malevolent spirits. And it is very likely that you would hear about great giants and their adventures. The North is rich with stories. However, if you gathered enough stories as you travelled from community to community, you would notice that one group of unique inhabitants is present in the folktales of every Arctic region—the little folk.

These diminutive inhabitants are hiding in all the remote places across the Arctic—high in the lonely mountains, away from people on the windswept tundra, and far out on the shifting sea ice. All of these places have known the footsteps and laughter of the little folk. In each region, these little beings are referred to by different names; however, many of the descriptions of their appearance and behaviour are very similar. We know that these little people are great hunters, and possess skills in toolmaking that exceed our own. They have a deep understanding of the land and weather, which gives them the ability to pass through rock and earth with ease, and to persuade the weather to change when needed.

But perhaps the greatest talent of the little folk is their ability to change their size. Consider for a moment how you might perceive the world if you could change your size at will. Who could intimidate you if you could match them in size with a simple thought? And if you could change your size so easily, what would be the size you would choose to remain for most of your day? You might answer that you would be a great giant with your head almost scraping the clouds. But think about it for another minute. Wouldn't the world seem small and confining if you were that large? I think that is why the little folk choose to be small. If you were small, the world would be a huge place with lots of space for everyone to live. Small rocks would seem like impressive boulders, and unremarkable cracks in the ground would become huge caverns where you could make a comfortable dwelling for your family. Do you see what I mean? For beings that are very small, the world is a magical place filled with mysteries that are missed by most of us.

As you read through this story, think about what I have said. These little Arctic folk might seem funny, and even silly, but if you listen closely, I think you will agree that these smallest of inhabitants are perhaps the most interesting race of magical beings in the Arctic.

Welcome to the world of the little folk!

Neil Christopher
Iqaluit, Nunavut, 2012

Ava pulled his old jacket close to his body. The wolverine fur trim on his hood, which would normally protect his face from the wind and blowing snow, was worn thin in places. When a gust of wind blew the hood off his head, Ava didn't bother to pull it back again. It wasn't providing much warmth anyway. The jacket was old and several sizes too big, and the winter wind easily found its way under his clothing to nip at his tender skin.

But Ava tried to ignore the wind's bite, as he always tried to ignore his pain and discomfort. Ava had seen other children cry to their mother or reach out for their father's hand when they fell or hurt themselves. But Ava didn't have anyone to reach out to. His parents had died when he was young. If he cried now, the adults in the village merely told him to be quiet. So, instead of worrying about the cold, he tried to just enjoy the sound of hard snow crunching under his feet at the old thule site.

Ava was happiest here, away from town and away from people. When he was alone at the thule site, he was safe from the insults and the shoves from all the unkind adults and children who made him feel unwelcome and unwanted.

This special place had become his place. He never understood why the other children did not visit the site, with its ring of rocks and old bowhead bones that marked ancient dwellings. Ava loved the old stones, which were mottled with orange and black lichen. In the summer, the ground was softer here. Mosses and grasses seemed to grow better in this place than anywhere else around town. He would often see lemmings darting here and there, making their homes under the old rocks and bones, or digging burrows into the thick humus. He wondered what it would be like to be a lemming, finding a warm home under any rock or in a small patch of earth.

As he climbed into one of the ancient dwellings and sat down, Ava tried to imagine the people who had lived here so many years ago. He thought that these people would have been kind to him. Maybe they would have adopted and protected him.

The faint rumble of snowmobile engines caught his attention. In the distance, Ava could see hunters from the town driving out towards the sea ice. Sleds trailed behind their snowmobiles. They were heading out onto the ice to find seal.

Every day he waved wildly, hoping that maybe that would be the day they would drive back and say, "Ava, you can follow! Hurry! Join us on the hunt!"

But today, like every day, the hunters drove past him. Either they did not notice Ava, or they chose to ignore him.

He stared at the hunters as they moved on and on towards the horizon. The rumble of the engines faded and the sleds slid farther and farther away, until they seemed like tiny dots in the distance.

"I don't need you!" Ava yelled after them, his voice cracking a little. The howling wind was the only response he received. "I'm fine out here alone!"

But just as he said this, Ava heard the snow crunch behind him, and realized that he was not alone after all.

He tried to control the panic rising inside him. Ava grabbed for the little knife at his side. It wasn't even a real knife, just a peg of wood that he'd sharpened so he would feel protected. But would a fake knife scare a bear? Or a wolf? Or whatever was behind him?

"Put that away," a voice commanded.

Ava gasped and spun around. He could see no one. He tightened his grip on the wooden peg and waved it vaguely in the direction of the voice.

"Who's there?" he said, trying to deepen his voice and stand as tall as he could. "Qinauvii? Who are you? Where are you hiding?"

He thought he heard a little giggle. The laugh wasn't menacing. Someone really found him funny.

"Where am I hiding? I think it's you who's hiding," the voice continued. And with that, a silhouette came into view. It looked like an old man kneeling in the snow, looking up at Ava.

The stranger had a smile on his bearded face. His eyes were neither threatening nor fearful.

Ava stepped towards the man hesitantly. Was he hurt? Why was he on his knees?

But as Ava moved closer to him, he realized that the stranger was not on his knees. He was only as tall *as* Ava's knees!

The man carried a tiny spear that wasn't even as long as Ava's forearm.

"What . . . are . . ." murmured Ava, frozen in his tracks. Then he remembered. An old woman in the village had told stories of magical little people who were great hunters, able to change their size at will. But Ava had only ever believed them to be stories.

"You . . . you're . . . you're a . . ." Ava stammered, blinking in disbelief.

"That's right," the tiny man said, stabbing the ground with his spear. "I'm a hunter."

"But you're so . . ." Ava's hands darted around in the air as he tried to find the words. The stranger's eyes followed the hand movements calmly. "You're so . . ."

"So well-dressed?" The man shrugged, stretching out his arm. "My wife is a talented seamstress."

As the hunter stretched out his arm, Ava saw miniature tools on the man's belt that looked like scraps of wire and tin.

The boy tried to stop staring. "But . . . no, this can't be."

"Well, all right, I admit," the hunter said, "I do some of the stitching myself. My wife may be a lot of things, but a fantastic tailor she's not. I was going hunting. You are welcome to follow."

With that, the man turned away from Ava, but motioned for the boy to come along.

Ava could not move for a moment. He had dreamed, so many times, that a hunter would appear and invite him along on a hunt. But never in the dream had the hunter been so small.

Ava swallowed hard and forced his own feet to move. He couldn't believe how quickly the little man travelled. His footprints were no bigger than the pawprints of a rabbit or the tracks of a small dog.

"But, how can you be a hunter?" Ava said, hoping his words would not offend the man. "You look, well, you know how you look."

"I find it hard to see myself," the small hunter grunted. "Why don't you tell me what you see?"

"You're . . . you're tiny!" Ava regretted the words as they escaped his lips.

The hunter paused again, and this time he turned his entire little frame towards Ava.

"One day you'll learn, tau, that a real man decides his own size. I am as big or as little as I choose to be. We all are."

Ava knew that word, "tau." The elders had said that this word was the name supernatural beings gave to Inuit. But did that mean this hunter was indeed one of the magical beings he had heard about in stories?

The boy's thoughts were interrupted by shouting in the distance and what sounded like a yelping pack of dogs. His instinct was to crouch or to hide, but the little hunter did not flinch.

"What's that?" Ava asked, trying not to let his voice tremble.

"Don't you know, tau? It's the sound of a hunt!"

Ava narrowed his eyes, trying to see through the blowing snow. He could see two dog teams heading towards them. Ava found it impossible to tell how far away the sleds were. How would he explain this magical being to these hunters?

But as the sleds approached, he realized they were not very far away at all. They were simply very small, just like the man in front of him. None of them was taller than Ava's knee. And they were accompanied by dogs that were the size of siksiks, the little ground squirrels that burrowed into the ground around town. These small dogs were attached to the sleds by tiny ropes that looked like braided sinew.

"Well, little tau, it looks like today's hunt is over. But tomorrow is a new day. If you still want to go for a hunt, tomorrow you will get your wish. Tomorrow you hunt with the Inugarulligaarjuit."

Inu-ga-ru-lli-gaar-juit. Ava remembered that word. It was what the old woman in the village had called the magical dwarves from Inuit legends—Inugarulligaarjuit!

"Go hunting? Yes, I would like that," Ava said, trying to keep his voice steady, as if this happened all the time. The other little hunters moved closer, showing no fear of Ava. "You're just different from the hunters from my village."

"That's right," said one of the little women who had just arrived. "We are different from your hunters." She craned her head to look up at Ava and added, "We actually catch things."

The other little folk laughed heartily, and Ava wasn't sure whether to smile or defend the hunters of his village. He wasn't sure if they would ever have defended him.

"Don't poke fun at him, Urju," the bearded man said to the woman. "He's had a tough day. They left him behind again."

"He's had a tough life, Sakku," one of the other hunters said, reaching out to untangle one of the dogs from its leads. Ava noticed that this hunter had only one eye and scars that ran along the side of his face. "And when hasn't he been left behind?"

Urju nodded as she practiced hurling a strangely shaped knife that was attached to a rope. "Well, now things will be different for him, Niigak."

Ava was growing uncomfortable. These beings seemed to know so much about him.

"I haven't had a tough life," Ava lied, defiantly. "I like my life."

9

Urju shook her head, taking the time to sit momentarily on the edge of a stone that was sticking out of the snow. "Of course you have, Ava. Which was your favourite part, getting teased or being forgotten?"

"How did you know I've been teased . . . wait a minute! How do you know my name?"

"Isn't it time someone knows who you are, Ava?" Urju answered, smiling as she began to sharpen the edge of her knife on the stone. It seemed as though the smile hid many stories. "So many questions from this one, Sakku. Perhaps it's time we fill that mouth with something other than questions."

She gestured towards the sleds, where three tiny seal carcasses were tied.

It did not look like much food at all, but Ava thought that perhaps the Inugarulligaarjuit did not eat much. Even thinking about food made his stomach grumble, and all the little hunters looked up, alarmed.

"You're right, Urju. It sounds as if the boy is hungry," Sakku said.

"It *sounds* like an avalanche waiting to happen," Urju muttered. That made Niigak laugh, and as he did so, the little dogs began to bark and wag their tails. It almost seemed as if the dogs understood the joke and were laughing along with him.

Ava held his stomach, embarrassed. He could not remember his last real meal.

"I think it is time that we go," Sakku announced, and the others nodded, moving towards the sleds. As Ava watched the little hunters preparing to leave, he suddenly felt like he was being abandoned all over again.

"No, wait. I'm sorry! Please don't leave me!" he exclaimed, sinking to his knees in the snow. When he did so, he was still taller than Sakku and Urju.

"Leave you?" Urju laughed. "Silly boy, no one is leaving you. You're coming with us."

Ava's eyes widened in disbelief. "I am?"

"Yes, Ava," Sakku continued, "you are coming home with us."

Home. Ava rolled the word around in his head for a moment. It was something so many of the children in the village took for granted. Ava was going to the home of the Inugarulligaarjuit! For the first time in his memory, Ava was excited to see what the future held for him.

So Ava began following the little group of hunters back to their home, stumbling behind as they led the way through the snow. He had to be careful not to lose them in the drifts, or worse, step on one of the dogs.

At last they reached an outcropping of rocks. As they neared the largest boulder, Ava thought he could hear drumming emanating from the rock. He trudged towards the rock with the hope of hearing where it was coming from.

Ava noticed that Niigak was untying the dogs. They crowded around the little hunter, as if they were his friends. This was something Ava had never felt himself.

"Niigak, do you need help with the dogs?" he asked shyly, wanting to somehow be useful.

Niigak looked up at the boy with his one eye. "The dogs and I are fine." He smiled. "They are happy to be home."

Home? Ava glanced around the rock for some sign of an iglu or shack, any dwelling at all, but he could see nothing. But then, stranger still, he started to hear voices coming from inside the rock.

Ava blinked in disbelief. His eyes searched along the rocky wall for some kind of door or opening. All he could see were minuscule cracks in the surface. But as he peered closer, he saw tiny breaks in the rock that almost resembled a doorway carved into the stone. And suddenly that doorway was pushed open from within!

13

Another little person emerged through the doorway. She looked older than Urju, and her greying, braided hair was decorated with little animal claws and feathers. And, to Ava's disbelief, she was not wearing boots or a jacket—her bare skin faced the cold wind without so much as a shiver.

"You're back at last!" she barked. Her sharp voice made Ava jump. "We weren't sure where you'd got to. Igimak won't be happy if he doesn't have seal for tonight's meal!"

Niigak, the hunter with one eye, let loose another booming laugh.

"When is Igimak ever happy, Aru? That's why you two get along so well. You both love to complain." He slapped her on the shoulder before vanishing into the open archway in the rock.

Aru growled like a wolf, but Ava thought he could see her smiling for a moment.

Sakku and Urju gathered their tools and followed Aru into the little tunnel as the dogs wandered in and curled up at the entrance.

Ava bent down to his hands and knees and peered inside. At first it was too dark to see anything. Then he noticed the flickering of a qulliq flame. As his eyes adjusted to the dim light, he could see the interior of the dwelling. It was beautiful. Thick furs lined the floors, while bags of seal oil leaned against the wall. Ava tried to recognize the strange skins on the walls, or the tools that hung below them, but there were many he had never seen before. He did recognize the smell of boiled seal and polar bear meat. And in the centre of the cavern: a fire that was no larger than Ava's thumb, yet seemed to bathe the entire dwelling in light.

"Well, come on in!" shouted Urju. "It isn't warmer with the door open!"

"Yes. Yes. I have set up a place for you to sleep," Sakku called back at him.

Ava gawked at the inviting sleeping platform, which was covered in warm furs. He had never imagined that he would have a chance to sleep on anything as nice as this.

But then, reality set in. Ava examined the miniature entrance tunnel. He knew there was no way he could fit into that little rock house.

"Thank you, Urju. Thank you, Sakku. But I can't get in there. You are both very kind, but this is no place for me."

Ava could feel his disappointment getting the better of him. His eyes had become watery and his throat felt tight. Before he became any sadder, one of the little huskies that had curled up by the entrance walked over and licked his cheek. The dog was in fact no bigger than Ava's hand, and this made the little orphan smile.

"Not tonight, eh?" Sakku said, as he stepped out of the little rock house and stood in front of Ava. "Well, it is up to you, but I hope you decide to come in soon. For tonight, I will make you a warm iglu to sleep in. Perhaps tomorrow you will change your mind about our home."

Confused, Ava watched the little hunter start to cut snow blocks from a nearby drift. Ava thought to himself, "What did he mean by saying that it was up to me? How could I ever fit inside that place?" So much of this day had been puzzling.

Very quickly, Sakku had shaped and built a solid iglu for Ava. Then he hurried back through the rock entrance. Moments later, he emerged with furs to line the iglu floor. Aru followed, walking barefoot through the snow to inspect Sakku's work, giving Sakku an occasional approving nod.

"This will keep the boy warm tonight," she said with a gap-toothed grin. "Now, let's make sure you get fed. Atii!" Another little man scurried out of the dwelling, carrying a large stack of seal meat. Ava was baffled to see it. Surely all this meat could not have come from the seals that he had seen the hunters bring home.

Ava sat down on the snow with a crunch. He quickly checked to make sure he hadn't sat down on one of the dogs, then he reached for the seal meat. Each portion looked very small in his hands.

Ava couldn't imagine how the tiny portions would feed him. What Igimak had piled high on the plate, he could swallow in one bite. But it was still more generous than any of the human villagers had ever been towards him.

The boiled seal meat was delicious, and he ate until his stomach would accept no more. He was surprised that these little pieces of meat from the tiny seal could fill him.

"I knew you'd love Igimak's food," Aru said, picking up the now-empty plate. "Cooking is his special gift. We all have one, you know. Everyone brings something different to our camp."

"Is your gift never getting cold?" Ava had to ask, hoping he didn't sound rude. He couldn't stop looking at her bare feet in the snow.

She laughed again and this time a hissing sound escaped from the gap between her teeth. "The Inugarulligaarjuit rarely get cold. But, yes, even amongst my kind I am especially comfortable in the snow."

"I would love to have a gift like yours, Aru. I can't see what I would bring to your village. I can't even fit inside the door."

Aru's face scrunched tightly and her lips twisted into a frown. She hopped towards him, leaping up on a pile of snow so she could look him in the eyes.

"Never say can't or won't, Ava. Here we say have not yet. What you are not able to do today might be something you can accomplish tomorrow." Her hand gently touched his shoulder. Strangely, Ava felt a surge of strength emanating through it.

"Look at me," Aru continued. "I was once in need of care and protection. And now I take care of this entire camp!"

"Enough talking! The boy must be tired!" Sakku said, as he emerged from the other side of the iglu. "You must sleep now," the little hunter added, speaking directly to Ava.

Aru nodded. "Get some rest. You are safe here."

Ava crouched on his stomach and crawled into the iglu. It was dark, but he was able to feel his way to the bed made of caribou skins. He carefully removed his outside clothing and crawled between the warm furs. Ava rested his head back against the thick pelt. He reflected on his strange and magical day.

He then heard the scraping and crunching sounds of footsteps tramping on the hard snow outside of his iglu. Sakku's head appeared in the entrance tunnel and he, too, crawled into the iglu. He was carrying something that was throwing light into the small space.

"I thought I would stay with you awhile, since it is your first night with us. And I brought my hunting qulliq. It is small, but it should give us some light and warmth."

Ava watched as Sakku placed the little lamp on a flat stone. The light from the flame caused shadows to dance around the iglu walls.

Ava noticed that three little huskies had followed Sakku into the iglu. They sniffed the fur bed and curled up next to Ava. Then Sakku closed his eyes and started singing a quiet song. The song was about a great man who had become lost at sea and paddled his kayak for many days on his journey home.

The quiet story-song, the dancing shadows, the whistling of wind outside, the warmth cast by the qulliq, and the little snoring huskies quickly put Ava into the most peaceful sleep he had ever known.

The next morning, Ava's eyes fluttered open. He was alone inside the iglu.

He could hear the dogs barking and whining in the camp. Sakku and the huskies were no longer in the iglu with him. The qulliq was gone and the iglu had cooled since the night before. He could see his breath condensing in the air in front of him. But the shelter had kept him warm and comfortable all night. It was the best sleep he could remember.

He slipped out of the furs, quickly dressed, and crawled out of the iglu. He saw that many members of the camp were already awake, tying the dogs to sleds and getting ready to go hunting.

"Good morning, Ava," Sakku said, as he readied a qamutiik.

"Good morning," Ava answered, again checking to make sure there were no dogs underfoot or nearby as he stepped. He was so excited to finally be going on a hunt.

"Are we going to hunt bear today?" Ava asked hopefully.

Sakku shook his head. "Not yet, little tau. Urju and Niigak will be hunting bear today," he said, pointing towards their packed sleds. "You and I will look for seal."

After a quick snack and some tea, Sakku and Ava headed out onto the sea ice. As they travelled on the ice, the dogs sniffed any bump or crack that might have been an aglu, a seal's breathing hole. Finally, they found two aglus close to one another. Sakku explained to Ava that he had to keep his feet very still, as the seal could feel the faintest vibrations on the ice.

"Now, place your harpoon on your feet. You need to remain still until you hear the sound of a seal breathing," Sakku explained. "When you hear this sound, grab your harpoon and drive it down into the hole. You will need to thrust hard and straight." With that, Sakku walked to the other aglu a short distance away and positioned himself.

Ava was excited at first, but he soon learned that he could not ask many questions, as they had to remain very still and very quiet. Ava was not good at being still or quiet. But Sakku could keep his tiny body completely motionless, the harpoon ready by his feet, waiting for the prey to emerge. Ava tried to do the same, but he did not have Sakku's patience.

"Do you notice sometimes, Ava, how a few minutes can feel like hours?" Sakku whispered, thoughtfully, without looking up from the aglu.

Ava realized that this was true. "Yes. When I'm doing something that I find difficult," he agreed. "But an hour can feel like a minute when I am doing something I enjoy."

Sakku smiled. "That's the way all things are in life. A second can feel like a minute, a minute like an hour. A tall man can seem small, a small man tall."

Ava thought about this the entire afternoon as they waited for a seal to appear. There were times when he looked across at Sakku and, poised with his harpoon, Sakku seemed almost the same height as the men in Ava's village. He wondered if this was a trick of the light on the snow, or if Sakku had changed size.

Ava's thoughts were interrupted by a chorus of barking dogs, punctuated by the cry of Niigak directing them. He looked up to see the Inugarulligaarjuit hunters on their way towards them.

Urju was running beside one of the sleds. Her face radiated excitement.

"Nanuq! Polar bear!" she exclaimed, breathlessly. "Just over the hill! I'm sure of it! There will be enough meat for the whole camp!"

Ava's heart beat faster, as this sounded much more exciting than waiting by a hole for a seal to finally emerge. But he didn't want to disappoint Sakku, so he tried to conceal his enthusiasm.

"What do you think, Ava? Should we follow Urju? Go after the bear?"

A giant grin broke across Ava's face and he nodded enthusiastically. Sakku yelled a command to the dogs and almost instantly they were up and running, a thunderous explosion of snow and sound, on the trail of the polar bear.

To Ava, they all appeared to be travelling at a remarkable speed. Very quickly he was out of breath from trying to keep up with his new friends. He paused for a minute to mop the sweat off his face. He still didn't understand how it was possible for them to move so fast with such little legs.

"Maybe little legs reach the ground faster," he thought to himself. But he then realized he had lost sight of the hunters.

Ava listened carefully, trying to remain still as Sakku had earlier, trying to hear where the party had gone. He struggled to locate the barks, as the sound seemed to be echoing off the snow and ice. At last, he was able to zero in on their position and he hurried in that direction.

As he charged on, excitement started to mingle with fear in his mind. He had heard the hunters in his village talk about huge white bears suddenly appearing in the white drift, like a phantom from nowhere, a sudden mass of claws and teeth, roaring. Those stories had plagued him in nightmares. Would a hidden bear pounce upon him? What if he could not fight it or escape it?

Never say can't, Ava! He heard Aru's voice in his head, reminding him to face the fears that sometimes seemed to loom so large.

Finally he saw the circle of hunters. The dogs were snapping and growling. Urju was twirling her roped weapon in the air. Niigak and Sakku had harpoons pointed, ready to lunge forward.

There was just one problem. Ava couldn't see a bear anywhere! What were they all pointing their weapons at?

He crept forward, not wanting to disturb the hunt. At the same time, he was terrified that this bear he was not able to see might strike out at any time.

And then Ava saw—right before him, surrounded by the hunters and dogs—a lemming. A chubby, little, white lemming!

Ava's mouth fell open. The Inugarulligaarjuit were indeed trying to surround the lemming, weapons ready, as if this was a dangerous animal.

And as he looked again, he realized the hunters were now smaller than before! They were almost the size of Ava's palm, facing the ferocity of one fat, growling lemming.

Urju was yelling orders at everyone. Niigak was trying to control the dogs. Sakku was crouching down, trying to find the perfect angle to launch his spear.

Urju was in the midst of yelling a
command when suddenly the lemming
charged at her. She was so busy telling
everyone what to do that she didn't
noticed it heading straight towards her.
But Ava saw it, and leapt forwards.

With one step, he crushed the lemming with his boot. But as he did this, something even stranger happened. The lemming's mouth opened wide and it growled like a polar bear. Large, jagged teeth tore away at his foot. But Ava did not move, and the lemming died under his kamik.

"Ava!" Urju exclaimed, a smile of gratitude on her face. "Thank you. You killed the bear!"

"Good work, Ava!" Sakku exclaimed. "Go back to camp and tell Aru and Igimak to get ready for a feast of bear!"

Ava was both proud and baffled. Normally he would never step on a lemming (even if it had seemed like a rather ferocious lemming). But why was this such an accomplishment? How would this one lemming be a feast for the whole camp?

Still, he did not want to disrespect his new friends. So Ava obeyed and returned to the camp, retracing his steps to where he had awoken that morning.

He found Aru waiting at the door, still in her simple clothes and bare feet.

"I killed a lemming . . . I mean, a bear. I caught a bear. We caught a bear. Igimak should prepare for a feast," he said simply.

Aru threw her head back and howled in approval. She hunched down, pried open the door on the side of the rock, and yelled down into the dwelling, "Nanuq!"

Ava heard Igimak scream in panic. Aru buried her head in one hand as she realized the mistake. "No, no, no, Igimak! A bear isn't attacking. They killed it. Ava killed it." She smiled her gap-toothed grin again, as Igimak let out a celebratory cheer. "So prepare for a feast! A huge feast indeed!" Igimak added.

Aru gestured behind Ava, towards the sleds that were led by the tired but still enthusiastic dogs.

Ava was amazed by what he saw.

The first sled appeared to be piled high with meat. How could all this meat have come from a lemming?

Then Ava saw Sakku's sled. There, lashed to the sled, was the white coat of a polar bear. Ava shook his head in disbelief, wondering if it was in fact the lemming's hide and his eyes were playing tricks on him. But, no. The thick coat, the long fur, the yellowish white colour, were definitely that of a polar bear.

"The lemming," he murmured. "I was . . . I was sure it was a lemming."

"Why are you so certain that a lemming *is* a lemming?" Aru whispered. "Humans do not have all the answers. Maybe what humans see as lemmings are really bears, and now you are seeing them for what they really are."

What was strange, however, was that Ava had stopped wondering how it was possible. He was simply filled with joy that the camp had so much meat, and that he had somehow helped. And what was even stranger was that the little hunters now seemed to be Ava's height.

Ava turned to say this to Aru and realized that not only were they the same size, but the door to the rock dwelling was now Ava's size as well.

"Aru!" he exclaimed. "The door . . . it grew."

"No, tau," Aru laughed. "It did not grow."

Ava gasped in amazement. "I shrunk?"

He felt Sakku's hand on his shoulder, the loving hand of an adoptive father who was proud of him. Ava felt that same surge of strength, like the one he'd felt when Aru reached out to him the night before.

"There is no shrinking or growing, Ava," Sakku said. "There is simply learning to see things in new ways."

"Like the door?"

"Like the door. The door to your new home," Sakku said, gesturing forwards.

And with that, Sakku led his newly adopted son into the enchanted camp, and into his new life with the Inugarulligaarjuit.

The End.

Contributors

Neil Christopher moved to Resolute Bay, Nunavut after teachers' college. He quickly fell in love with the North and has made it his home. It was during his first few years in the North that Neil was introduced to the rich mythology of the Inuit. For the last ten years, Neil has been researching Inuit myths and legends and has published books and directed films on the topic for children, youth, and adults.

Alan Neal is a Canadian journalist and playwright whose first project involving the creatures of Inuit myth was on a film Neil Christopher was making in Iqaluit years ago about the supernatural being Mahaha. Alan's tasks then included coaching child actors, wrangling dogs, and performing the role of Grip #3. Although the film never did get finished, Alan fell in love with both the stories and the beauty of Iqaluit. He currently hosts the CBC radio program *All in a Day* in Ottawa, and has also hosted the programs *Ontario Today*, *Bandwidth*, and *Fuse*. He is thrilled and honoured that Inhabit Media invited him to try his hand at co-writing a story based on Inuit folklore.

Jonathan Wright is an illustrator and animator living in Iqaluit, Nunavut. He graduated from Sheridan College in Ontario and has illustrated for a variety of newspapers, magazines, and books.

Character Names *

NAME	PRONUNCATION	MEANING
Aru	*ah-roo*	No known meaning
Ava	*a-va*	Shore spirit
Igimak	*ig-ee-mack*	Specialized spear
Niigak	*Nee-gak*	The action of snaring something
Sakku	*Sak-koo*	Harpoon point
Urju	*or-jew*	Ground vegetation or sod

* NOTE TO READER: *Most Inuit names have a meaning. They could describe an object, action, or animal.*

Glossary

NAME	PRONUNCIATION	MEANING
Aglu	*ag-loo*	Breathing hole in sea ice used by animals
Atii	*a-tee*	Command, "to go" or "hurry up"
Iglu	*ig-loo*	Dwelling made with snow blocks
Inugarulligaarjuit	*in-new-ga-roo-lee-ga-jew-eet*	Supernatural race of little beings
Kamiik	*kam-eek*	Boots made of animal skin
Nanuq	*nan-uk*	Polar bear
Qamutiik	*kam-oo-teek*	Traditional sled
Qulliq	*koo-lik*	Traditional stone lamp
Thule	*too-lee*	An Inuit culture that existed 500–1500 years ago
Qinauvii	*key-now-vee*	"Who are you?"
Tau	*t-ow*	Term used by supernatural beings to refer to an Inuit person

Inhabit Media Inc. would like to acknowledge the support of the
Qikiqtani Inuit Association (QIA). Without their generous support this
publication would not have been possible.

Published by Inhabit Media Inc.
www.inhabitmedia.com

Nunavut Office: P.O. Box 11125, Iqaluit, Nunavut, X0A 1H0
Ontario Office: 146A Orchard View Blvd., Toronto, Ontario, M4R 1C3

Editors:	Louise Flaherty, Kelly Ward, and Alethea Arnaquq-Baril
Written by:	Neil Christopher and Alan Neal
Art Direction by:	Neil Christopher
Illustrations by:	Jonathan Wright

Design and layout copyright © 2012 by Inhabit Media Inc.
Text copyright © 2012 by Neil Christopher and Alan Neal
Illustrations copyright © 2012 by Inhabit Media Inc. and Jonathan Wright

We acknowledge the support of the Canada Council for the Arts for our
publishing program.

ISBN 9781-927095-02-7

Printed and bound in Hong Kong by Paramount Printing Co. • September 2013 • #135989

Library and Archives Canada Cataloguing in Publication

Christopher, Neil
 Ava and the little folk / written by Neil Christopher and Alan
Neal ; illustrated by Jonathan Wright.

ISBN 978-1-927095-02-7

 I. Christopher, Neil, 1972-
II. Wright, Jonathan, 1978- III. Title.

PS8627.E21A83 2012   jC813'.6   C2012-900592-4

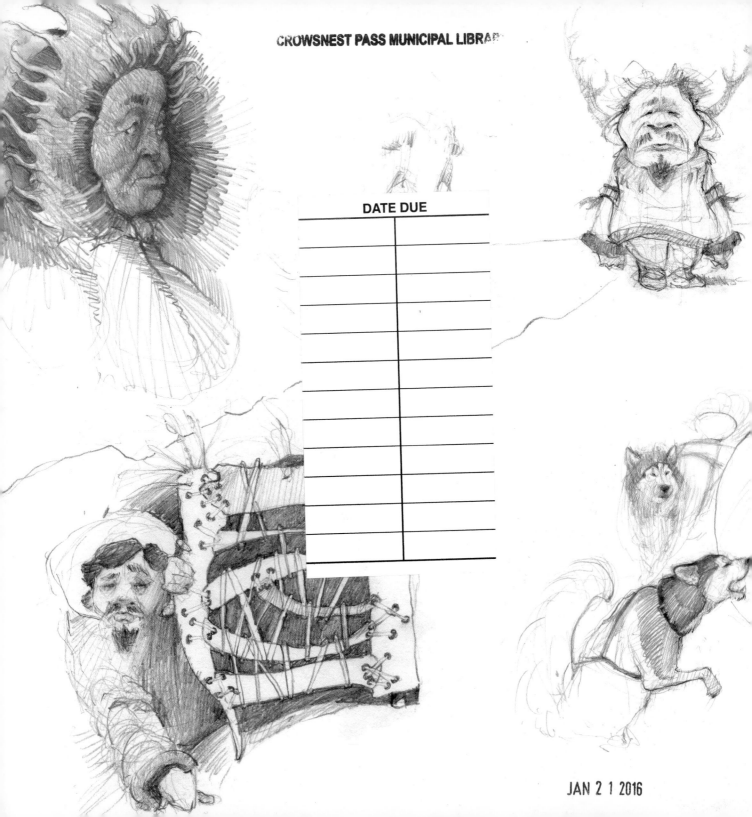

DATE DUE